Story

I can read the Speed sounds.

I can read the Green words.

I can read the Red words.

I can read the story.

I can answer the questions about the story.

I can read the Speed words.

Story  Rag the rat

Say the Speed sounds

Consonants

Ask your child to say the sounds (not the letter names) clearly and quickly, in and out of order. Make sure he or she does not add 'uh' to the end of the sounds, e.g. ' f' not 'fuh'.

f	l	m	n	r	s	v	z	sh	th	ng nk

b	c k ck	d	g	h	j	p	qu	t	w	x	y	ch

Each box contains one sound.

Vowels

Ask your child to say each vowel sound and then the word, e.g. 'a' 'at'.

at	hen	in	on	up

Read the Green words

For each word ask your child to read the separate sounds, e.g. 'r-a-t', 'w-i-th' and then blend the sounds together to make the word, e.g. 'rat', 'with'. Sometimes one sound is made up of more than one letter, e.g. 'th', 'sh', 'ck'. These are underlined.

rat with his big top hat

it and up a bat clap

cat mat flap

Ask your child to read the root word first and then the word with the ending.

rap → raps tap → taps pop → pops

Read the Red words

Red words don't sound like they look. Read the word out to your child. Explain that he or she will have to stop and think about how to say the red word in the story.

the

Story 1

Rag the rat

Introduction

Have you ever seen a magician? This rhyming story is about a magician who is a rat. What do you think he might pull out of his hat?

Rag the rat
with his big top hat,

raps it, taps it,
and up pops a bat.

Clap, clap, clap!

Ask your child:

What does Rag the rat do to his hat to make magic?

Rag the rat
with his big top hat,

raps it, taps it,
and up pops a cat.
Clap, clap, clap!

Rag the rat
with his big top hat,
raps it, taps it,
and up pops a mat.

Flap, flap, flap!

Ask your child:

What three things pop out of Rag's hat?

Speed words for Story 1

Ask your child to read the words across the rows, down the columns and in and out of order, clearly and quickly.

clap	big	mat	pops	up
bat	and	the	hat	taps
it	cat	raps	a	top
his	with	clap	rat	flap

Story 

I can read the Speed sounds. 

I can read the Green words. 

I can read the Red words. 

I can read the story. 

I can answer the questions about the story. 

I can read the Speed words. 

Story  Jess in a mess

Say the Speed sounds

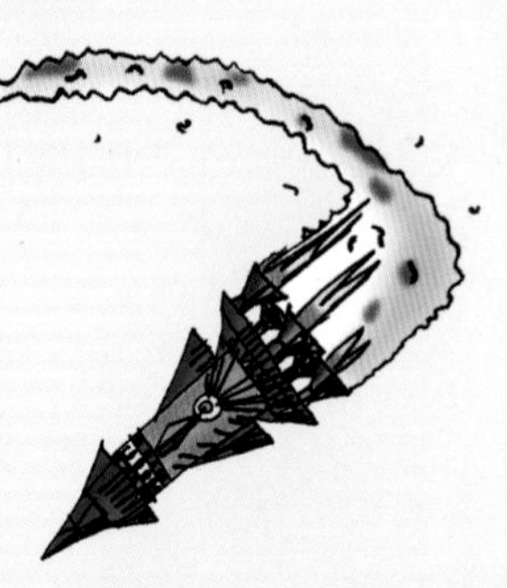

Consonants

Ask your child to say the sounds (not the letter names) clearly and quickly, in and out of order. Make sure he or she does not add 'uh' to the end of the sounds, e.g. 'f' not 'fuh'.

f	l	m	n	r	s ss	v	z	sh	th	ng nk

b	c k ck	d	g	h	j	p	qu	t	w	x	y	ch

Each box contains one sound.

Vowels

Ask your child to say each vowel sound and then the word, e.g. 'a' 'at'.

at	hen	in	on	up

Read the Green words

For each word ask your child to read the separate sounds, e.g. 'm-u-d', 's-p-l-a-sh' and then blend the sounds together to make the word, e.g. 'mud', 'splash'. Sometimes one sound is made up of more than one letter, e.g. 'th', 'sh', 'nk'. These are underlined.

in mud and splash a big

mess but big trunk is

just thing off

Ask your child to read the root word first and then the word with the ending.

hop → hops sit → sits

skip → skips slip → slips

Read the Red words

Red words don't sound like they look. Read the words out to your child. Explain that he or she will have to stop and think about how to say the red words in the story.

she the to

Story 2

Jess in a mess

Introduction

Do you like elephants? This rhyming story is about an elephant who keeps getting dirty.

Jess hops in mud.

She sits in mud.

She skips and slips and trips in mud.

Splash!

Ask your child:

What five things does Jess do in the mud?

Jess gets in a
big, big mess.

But Mum's big trunk
is just the thing

to get the mud off Jess.

Splash!

Ask your child:

What does Jess's mum use her trunk for?

Speed words for Story 2

Ask your child to read the words across the rows, down the columns and in and out of order, clearly and quickly.

mud	big	just	hops	she
trunk	to	skips	sits	thing
splash	slips	mess	in	gets
trips	and	the	off	but